Ooey-gooey
Animals

Ooey-gooey
Animals 123

Lola Schaefer

www.raintreepublishers.co.uk

Visit our website to find out more information about **Raintree** books.

To order:

☎ Phone 44 (0) 1865 888112

🖹 Send a fax to 44 (0) 1865 314091

💻 Visit the Raintree Bookshop at www.raintreepublishers.co.uk to browse our catalogue and order online.

First published in Great Britain by Raintree, Halley Court, Jordan Hill, Oxford OX2 8EJ, part of Harcourt Education.
Raintree is a registered trademark of Harcourt Education Ltd.

Editorial: Nick Hunter and Diyan Leake
Design: Sue Emerson (HL-US) and Joanna Sapwell
Picture Research: Amor Montes de Oca (HL-US)
Production: Lorraine Hicks

Originated by Dot Gradations
Printed and bound in China by South China Printing Company

ISBN 1 844 21026 X
07 06 05 04 03
10 9 8 7 6 5 4 3 2 1

British Library Cataloguing in Publication Data
Schaefer, Lola
Ooey-gooey Animals 123
513.2'11
A full catalogue record for this book is available from the British Library.

Acknowledgements
The publishers would like to thank the following for permission to reproduce photographs: Corbis pp. 3, 5 (Gallo Images), **23** (sucker, Gallo Images), back cover (sucker, Gallo Images); Dwight Kuhn pp. **9**, **19**, **23** (bristles); Graeme Teague pp. **15**, **22**; Jay Ireland & Georgienne Bradley/bradleyireland.com p. **11**; Photovault pp. **17**, **21** (Wernher Krutein), **23** (tentacles), back cover (tentacles); Visuals Unlimited pp. **7** (William C. Jorgensen), **13** (Bill Beatty), **23** (mucus, Bill Beatty)

Cover photographs of a newt and earthworms, reproduced with permission of Dwight Kuhn; photograph of jellyfish reproduced with permission of Photovault (Wernher Krutein)

Every effort has been made to contact copyright holders of any material reproduced in this book. Any omissions will be rectified in subsequent printings if notice is given to the publishers.

CAUTION: Remind children that it is not a good idea to handle wild animals. Children should wash their hands with soap and water after they touch any animal.

Some words are shown in bold, **like this.** You can find them in the glossary on page 23.

One 1

One jellyfish moves in the deep water.

Two 2

Leeches have two **suckers**.

1

2

suckers

Three 3

Three sea slugs swim
in the ocean.

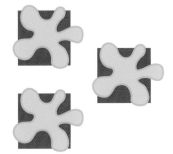

Four 4

Earthworms use their stiff **bristles** to move along the ground.

Here are four bristles.

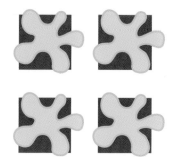

bristles

1   2   3   4

Five 5

Five earthworms crawl across the ground.

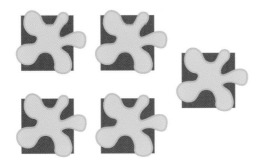

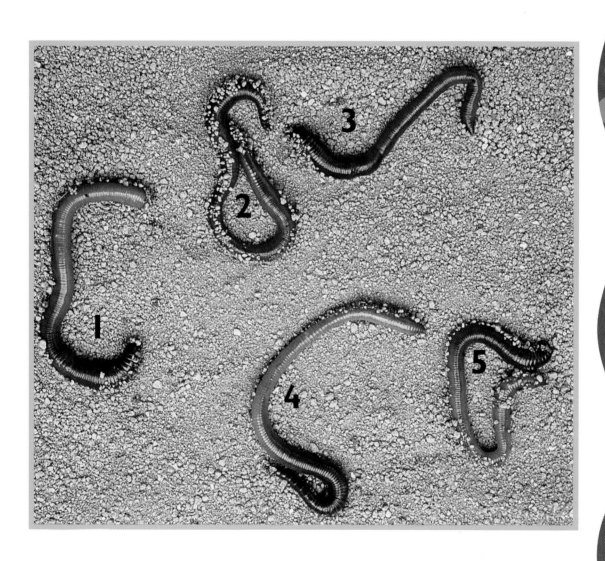

Six 6

Six newts have gooey
mucus on their body.

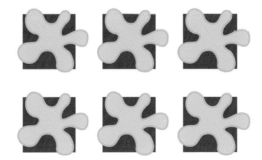

Seven 7

Seven sea anemones look like flowers in the ocean.

Eight   8

You can see eight **tentacles** on this jellyfish.

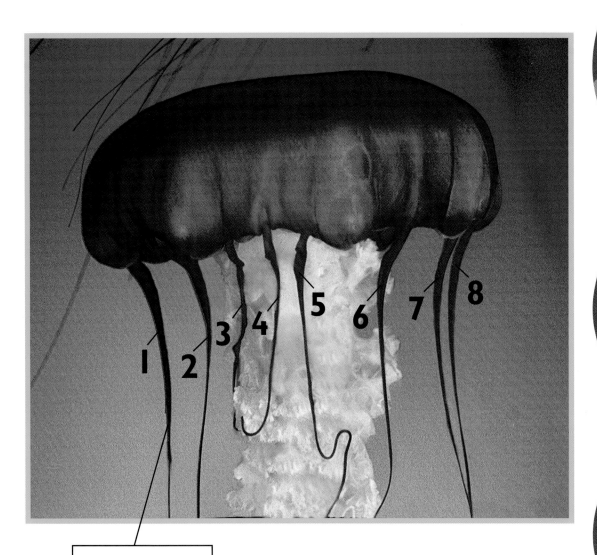

tentacle

Nine   9

This slug has laid nine eggs.

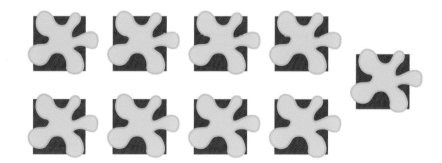

Ten 10

These ten jellyfish have long **tentacles**.

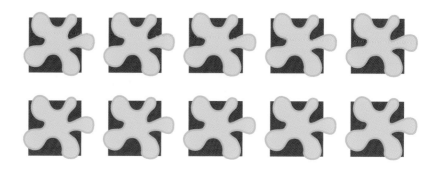

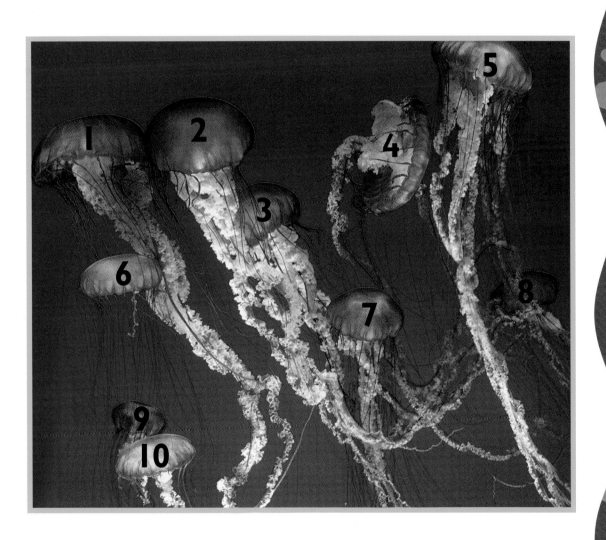

Look closely!

How many sea anemones can you count on the rock?

Look for the answer on page 24.

Glossary

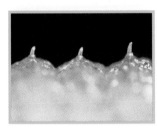

bristles
short, stiff hairs

mucus
slimy stuff that some animals have in or on their body

sucker
part of an animal's body which it uses to stick to other things

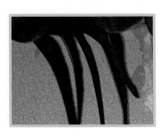

tentacles
long, thin parts that some animals have on their body

Index

bristles   8, 9, 23

earthworms   8, 10

eggs   18

jellyfish   3, 16, 20

leeches   4

mucus   12, 23

newts   12

ocean   4, 14

sea anemones   14, 22

slugs   6, 18

suckers   4, 5, 23

tentacles   16, 17, 23

water   3

Answer to quiz on page 22
There are eight sea anemones
on this rock.

Titles in the Ooey-gooey Animals series include:

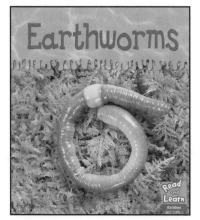

Hardback   1 844 21020 0

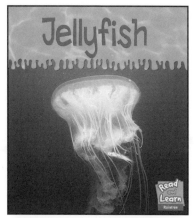

Hardback   1 844 21021 9

Hardback   1 844 21022 7

Hardback   1 844 21023 5

Hardback   1 844 21024 3

Hardback   1 844 21025 1

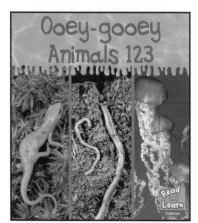

Hardback   1 844 21026 X

Find out about the other titles in this series on our website www.raintreepublishers.co.uk